Postman Pat
Makes a Present

Story by **John Cunliffe**   *Pictures by* **Jane Hickson**

from the original Television designs by **Ivor Wood**

Hippo

"What a lot of cards and letters!" said Pat.
"That's because it's Mother's Day on Sunday," said Mrs. Goggins.
"Oh," said Pat. "I'd forgotten. I'd better get a card for my old mum."
"And a nice present," said Mrs. Goggins.
"I wonder what she'd like?" said Pat.

Pat was on his way.
He called on Mrs. Pottage at Greendale Farm.

"Did you know?" said Pat. "It's Mother's Day on Sunday."

"Of course," said Mrs. Pottage. 'I'm sending my mother a box of hankies."

"My mum has a drawer full of hankies," said Pat.

Pat was on his way.
He met Dr. Gilbertson along the road.

9

"Did you know?" said Pat. "It's Mother's Day on Sunday."

"Of course," said Dr. Gilbertson. "I'm giving my mum a book."

"Mine only reads the Bible," said Pat, "and she already has three."

Pat was on his way.
He called on Ted Glen. Ted was very busy.

"Did you know?" said Pat. "It's Mother's Day on Sunday."
"Of course," said Ted. "I'm fettling this clock for my dear old mother."
"My mum has six clocks," said Pat, "and they all go."

15

Pat was on his way.
He called on Granny Dryden.

"Did you know?" said Pat. "It's Mother's Day on Sunday, and I have no idea what to give my mother."

"I know what she'll like best," said Granny Dryden. "She'll like something that you've made."

"I could knit her a jumper," said Pat. "But it would never be ready in time."

"Not a jumper," said Granny Dryden. "Make her a simnel cake."

"A what?" said Pat.

"A simnel cake. That's what everybody made in the old days. It's a fruit-cake, with lots of marzipan on top. Nice and spicy. She'll know. Like the old times."

"That's what I'll do," said Pat.

Pat baked his cake after tea. There was a lovely smell in the kitchen.

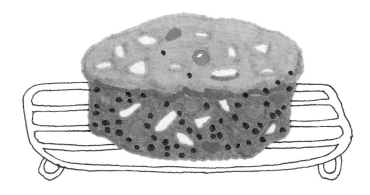

"Make one for us as well," said Sara. "It smells good."

So he did.

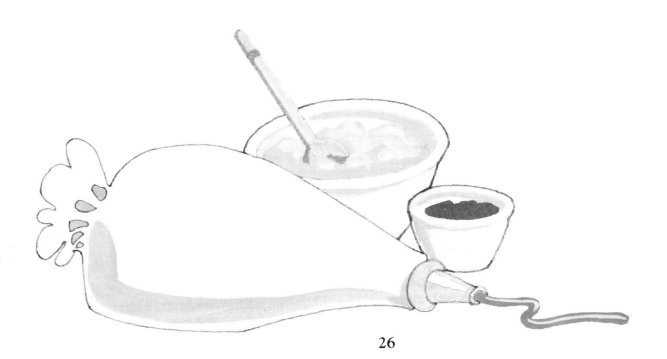

Pat and Sara and Julian all went to see Pat's old mother on Mothering Sunday. They took some flowers from the garden and the simnel cake.

She was very pleased to see them. They all had a slice of the cake with a cup of tea.
It was delicious.

"Just right for Mother's Day," said Pat's mother. "Just like the old times."